By George Gr

Illustrated by Nidhom (iNDOS

Toby, The Laughing Hyena Who Lost His Sense Of Humor

Everyone knows that animals have excellent hearing abilities. For most of them, being able to hear well helps them to stay alive. Different animals make different sounds, but often the sounds they make can't be heard by humans. This is because they talk to each other on what's called a *higher frequency level*. Have you ever heard the sound that comes from a dog whistle? Of course not. The whistle sound is out of *our* hearing range, but fits just right in a dog's!

This story starts out with a character you may have already met, Lenny the Lion.
He was the king of the jungle and he had a very important message that needed to be heard by each and every animal in his kingdom.

He called out to the animals, saying that there was to be an emergency meeting in the center of the jungle. He said that everyone was to join and that it was to be a peaceful meeting, with no fighting or arguing.

You see... Lenny had a very
special friend, Toby the Hyena,
and poor Toby had
a very serious problem.

"Spread the word to all the creatures in the jungle, big and small," called Lenny. "My friend, Toby, needs some help." Because Lenny was the king, and a really nice king he was, everyone listened to him.

The birds flew overhead and called to the elephants, monkeys, zebras, baboons, porcupines, wild horses, giraffes, bees and even some fish who'd be able to swim upstream to get to the meeting place in the jungle. "Come quickly," they called.
"Run, fly, walk, swim... whatever it takes, just be there."

Before long the message had spread throughout the jungle. "The king of the jungle has told us to be there, so be there we *will*," said all the animals to each other.

Sonny, a lovely girl hyena, told her friends to get ready to go.
She thought she might be the only one able to help Toby.
None of the animals knew what was wrong with him, but
all Sonny knew was that she loved him and if he had a
problem, she was going to do her very best to try and help.

My goodness!
This was to be a day
that everyone would
remember.

Every bird of every kind headed
over the jungle, in the sky,
toward the meeting place.
All the animals with four legs ran their hearts out,
crashing through
trees and jumping
over logs to get there.
Snakes slithered, bees buzzed, frogs leaped, fish swam —
all of them as fast as they could, to get to the center
of the jungle.

Wow! What a sight!
Some even wondered if there'd be enough
room for everyone.

In the center of the meeting place, in the center of the jungle, sat Lenny the Lion King on his grand high chair.
His crown sparkled in the sunlight.
Next to him, in another chair, sat Toby the Hyena.
It didn't take long for everyone to become quiet as they noticed his sad face.
What was the problem?
Lenny was about to tell them.

"As you all know, there are times when we are enemies and we get into terrible fights. But the rest of the time we are friends. We eat together, play together and sleep close by each other. There are also times when our friends need help and we do our best to give it to them. Well, this is one of those times!

My friend, Toby the Hyena, is known for his laughter and his giggle. This is why the world knows him as *Toby the Laughing Hyena*. From the time he was born he giggled and laughed, and seemed to be the happiest animal in the jungle. But now, my friends, Toby no longer laughs. He eats and drinks and walks around, but has not laughed in weeks. Because I am the king, he came to me and asked me for help. I feel very sorry for poor Toby. This is why I made the decision to call you all together.

I hope that someone might be able to make him laugh again.
I know there are many of you that would
like to try. So, now that you know why you're
here, come forward. Come as close to
Toby as you want. Try to make him
laugh. I promise something very
special to the one who succeeds.
Okay... who wants to be
the first to try?"

Zamba the Zebra stepped forward. "I'll try. I have
something to tell Toby. It might make him laugh."
As Toby looked down at the ground, with no smile, and
the other animals kept still, Zamba asked Toby a question.

"Toby, do you know why zebras can't play card games
in the jungle?"
Toby continued to look at the ground and said,
"No, Zamba, I don't."
Zamba then gave him the answer.
"Because there're too many
cheetahs around!"

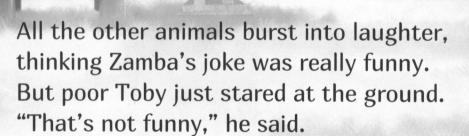

All the other animals burst into laughter,
thinking Zamba's joke was really funny.
But poor Toby just stared at the ground.
"That's not funny," he said.
The animals went still again as Zamba walked away
from Toby's side.

"I'll try next," came a voice from behind an elephant.
It was Peter the Porcupine. He walked up to Toby and said,
"Toby... do you know how porcupines kiss
and hug each other?"
"No," said Toby without lifting
his head. Peter gave him the
answer. "*Very* carefully!"
Again the animals began to
laugh loudly and some even
clapped, thinking Peter was a super funny guy.
But Toby just stared at the ground. "That's not funny,"
he said. Peter turned
and walked away as
the other
animals sighed.

Then Manny the Monkey swung down to Lenny from a tree. "Can I have a turn?" "Of course," said Lenny, "do your best." Manny held a banana in each hand, and then stood in front of Toby.

"Toby, what do you call a monkey with a banana in each ear?" Toby just huffed and said, "What?" Manny stuffed a banana in each of his ears and said, "Anything you want, it wouldn't hear you!"

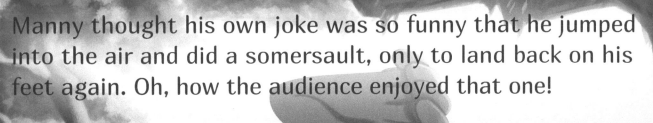

Manny thought his own joke was so funny that he jumped into the air and did a somersault, only to land back on his feet again. Oh, how the audience enjoyed that one!

They all clapped
and laughed until tears
formed in their eyes!
But Toby just sat
in his chair and said,
"*Nope*, not funny."

"Oh, come on..." said Manny,
"... that one was good."
Toby looked Manny in the
eyes and said, "*NOT* funny."
Slowly Manny took a few
steps backwards and then
scampered back to his tree.
The audience couldn't believe
that Toby hadn't found his joke
funny at all. Toby really did have
a problem, poor guy.

Ely the Elephant then stomped over to Toby.
"*I can do this...*" he whispered to Lenny as he winked at him. Lenny smiled and whispered back, "*Go on then.*"
Ely looked at Toby and asked, "Toby, what do you give an elephant with feet like mine?"
"What?" said Toby refusing to look up.

Ely began stomping around the place as he answered, "Plenty of *room*!"
The other animals leaped backwards as Ely got closer to them. Some of them even tripped over because they had the giggles and couldn't walk straight!
But again Toby said, "I'm not laughing. That wasn't funny."
"Oh dear," said a few of the animals. No one knew what to do now, none of them had anymore jokes to tell.

After a moment of quiet, Henry the Hummingbird flew up to Toby and sat comfortably on his shoulder.

"Toby," he said. But Toby just let out a disgruntled moan.
"Do you know why hummingbirds hum?"
"No, I don't," said Toby.

Henry flew off Toby's shoulder and hovered right in front of his sad-looking face and said, "Because they don't know the words!"

The audience watched Toby closely. Henry's joke just *had* to make him smile, even just a little.

But, "Sorry," said Toby. "That just wasn't funny to me."

The whole time, Sonny had been watching Toby from behind a bush. She didn't like seeing him so down. It was her turn now, and she really hoped that what she would say might cheer him up. She walked over to him and then sat down by his side. She leaned over and began to whisper something in his ear.

What do you know? As Sonny pulled away Toby looked up and, from nowhere, the most amazing smile formed across his face.

The animals *gasped*. What had Sonny said?

Suddenly Toby began to giggle. Then his giggle turned into a laugh, then his laugh turned into a really loud cackle... until... he was too weak to even sit straight anymore.

He was laughing harder now than he ever had before.

Like the audience, Lenny was curious. "Toby, please tell us what Sonny said. Her joke must have been really funny." Toby pulled himself together, calmed down slightly and then said, "She didn't tell me a joke at all. She said that if I could find it within myself to laugh again... she'd marry me. I then realized what a fool I was for being so down, and I remembered all the jokes that have been told to me today."

He began laughing again, "and now... *ha ha ha heh heh... I can't... heh heh ha ha... stop... heh he ha... laughing... ha ho ho ho hehe hee...!*"

"Hooray,"
cheered all the animals...
"Hooray for you, Sonny!"

Good old Sonny just smiled
as Toby gave her a kiss
on the cheek.

The next day the meeting place in the jungle looked more beautiful than it ever had. Toby and Sonny were getting married! And who do you think performed the ceremony? Yup... of course... Lenny, the King of the Jungle, married the laughing hyenas. When Lenny finally said, "I now declare you husband and wife..." the jungle animals *woohoo'd* and *hooray'd* until they ran out of breath!

Lenny then turned to Sonny. "Remember, Sonny, I promised a special gift to the one who made Toby laugh. So, your special gift is... any honeymoon you want... in my kingdom. Ely here will ride you both wherever you want to go. It's my special way of saying thank you for helping Toby to find his sense of humor." Of course Sonny was pleased. She and Toby jumped onto Ely's back and prepared to ride into the sunset, with a *'just married'* sign stuck to Ely's behind.

What a day, *what a day!*

Our little story shows us that when friends feel down,
it's important to try to make them laugh.
Why? Because laughter, after all, is the best medicine!
Our story also shows us that just a little love
can really change a person.
Keep this in mind as you grow older;
love and laughter can fix just about any problem!

THE END

Fun Facts
For You

Hyenas are one of the oldest animal species found on Planet Earth today. Scientific evidence shows that hyenas have been in existence for over twenty-two-million years.

Hyenas are well-known for their vocal abilities.
They communicate to one another in cackles and laughs,
which often sound like a person giggling.
They are also known for their powerful jaws;
their bite can come down at a pressure of 800lbs per inch.
This is why hyenas are often referred to as
'bone-crushers'.

Like some other animals, Hyenas will at some time in their lives separate from their families. They do this to go in search of another hyena, boy or girl, in hope of starting their own family. Once they have formed a pack, they will hunt together and keep close to one another.

Spotted Hyenas were known to be kept as pets in the ancient times. Hyenas are found throughout most of Africa and in some parts of Asia.

While hyenas are usually afraid of male lions, due to their awesome strength, they have been known to attack lionesses. Lionesses generally live in fear of hyenas, especially when they approach in a pack. The lionesses know that hyenas have extremely powerful jaws and, like any mother or mother-to-be; she *knows* she must protect herself and her family.

Fun For You!
Animal Jokes To Make You Laugh

WHY DO LIONS EAT RAW MEAT?

Because they don't know how to cook

HOW DOES A FROG FEEL WHEN HE BREAKS HIS FOOT?

Unhoppy

WHY SHOULD YOU BE CAREFUL WHEN IT'S RAINING CATS AND DOGS?

You don't want to step in the poodles

WHAT KIND OF BEES LIVE NEAR GRAVEYARDS?

Zom-bees

WHY CAN'T LEOPARDS HIDE WELL?

Because they're always spotted

WHAT DO YOU CALL A SLEEPING BULL?

A bull-dozer

WHY ARE FISH SO CLEVER?

Because they live in schools

HOW DOES A COW FARMER COUNT HIS HERD?

He uses his cow-culator

WHAT DO CATS EAT FOR BREAKFAST?

Mice Krispies

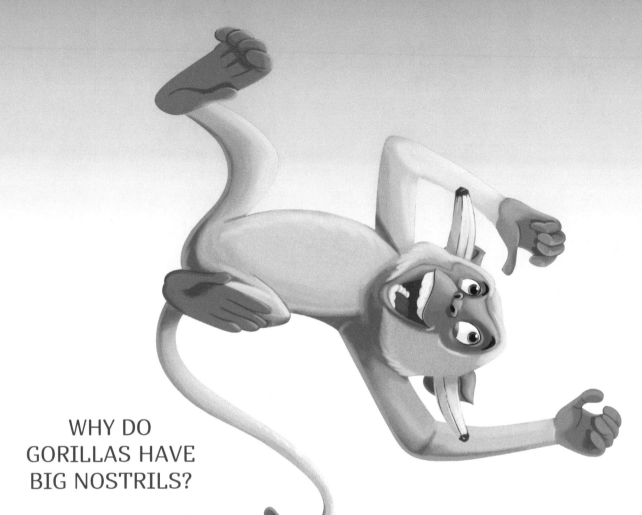

WHY DO
GORILLAS HAVE
BIG NOSTRILS?

Because they have big fingers

WHY ARE TEDDY BEARS
NEVER HUNGRY?

Because they're always stuffed

WHAT IS A CAT'S
FAVORITE COLOR?

Purr-ple

WHAT DO BEES LIKE
TO SIT ON?

Their bee-hinds

WHY DO COWS WEAR
BELLS?

Because their horns don't work

WHAT HAPPENED TO THE
CAT WHO SWALLOWED
A BALL OF WOOL?

She had mittens

WHERE DO COWS LIKE TO
GO WITH THEIR FRIENDS?

To the mooovies

HOW DO YOU CATCH A MONKEY?

Climb a tree and act like a banana

WHAT'S WORSE THAN AN ALLIGATOR COMING TO DINNER?

Two alligators coming to dinner

WHAT DO YOU CALL THE TOP OF A DOGHOUSE?

A woof

WHAT DO YOU CALL A COW IN AN EARTHQUAKE?

A milkshake

HOW DO YOU STOP A CHARGING ELEPHANT?

You take away its credit card

WHY DID THE MAN THROW THE BUTTER OUT THE WINDOW?

He wanted to see a butter-fly

WHAT'S A CAT'S FAVORITE NURSERY RHYME?

Three blind mice

WHAT DO YOU CALL A DOG THAT CAN TELL THE TIME?

A watchdog

WHAT DO YOU CALL A COW THAT LIVES IN AN IGLOO?

An eskimooo

Acknowledgements

This book was the most fun book to write. Our team laughed throughout the creative process.

A big thank you goes to Carly van Heerden, my good South African friend. Her editing was essential in the completion of my writings.

A good book requires great illustrations. Indeed we have them thanks to Nidhom (iNDOS Studios), our very talented Indonesian illustrator.

Every product needs finishing touches. Xenia Janicijevic-Jovic, our team book designer working out of Serbia, added additional sparkle to the concept and content of Toby, The Laughing Hyena Who Lost His Sense Of Humor.

The biggest thank you goes to my son, Randy Green. His expertise in on-demand publishing, and ability to find the right people for me to work with (regardless of where they are in the world), are simply amazing and sincerely appreciated. He knows how to make a father happy!

George

Toby, The Laughing Hyena Who Lost His Sense Of Humor

By George Green

First Printing, 2014

Printed in the USA
CPSIA information can be obtained
at www.ICGtesting.com
LVHW060333040124
768126LV00002B/17